For Chris: A treasured friend in all seasons.

—Karen

To the sweetest wilderness!

—Marc

Library of Congress Cataloging-in-Publication Data available.

ISBN 978-1-7972-1503-7

Manufactured in China.

Design by Ryan Hayes.
Typeset in Goldenbook and Lake Informal.
The illustrations in this book were rendered digitally.

10 9 8 7 6 5 4 3 2 1

Chronicle Books LLC
680 Second Street
San Francisco, California 94107

Chronicle Books—we see things differently.
Become part of our community at www.chroniclekids.com.

Wake Up, Woodlands

by Karen Jameson

pictures by Marc Boutavant

chronicle books · san francisco

Wake up, *Tiny Whiskers.*

No more storming

Woods are warming

Sweep your sleepy dreams away.

Scamper out to meet the day.

Wake up, *Little Buzz.*

No gray looming

Buds are blooming

Shake the winter from each wing.

Blossom-hopping starts in spring.

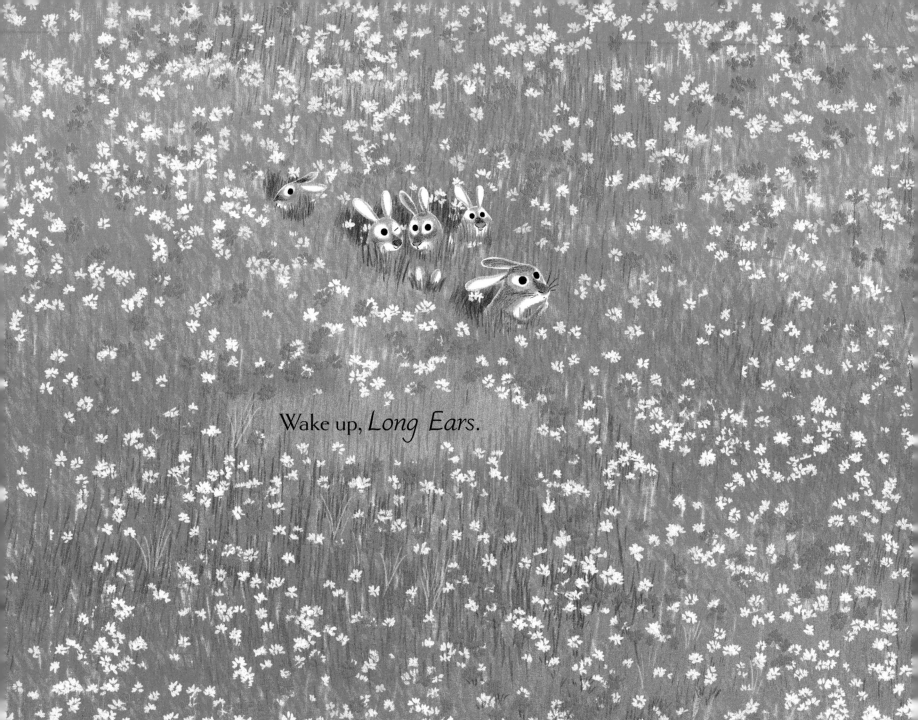

Wake up, *Long Ears*.

Winter's over

Field's in clover

One more snuggle—stretch and yawn.

Bound outdoors to greet the dawn.

Wake up, *Small Paws.*

No more snowing

Streams are flowing

Breakfast's waiting, little one.

Catch your trout in morning sun.

Wake up, *Bright Wings*.

No more freezes

Gentle breezes

Wriggle free of your cocoon.

Float through fields of spring perfume.

Wake up, *Big Eyes*.

Frost is fading

Spring's parading

Peek out from your hiding places.

Graze with Mom in grassy spaces.

Wake up, *Chubby Cheeks.*

Ice is thawing

Time for gnawing

Leap around from tree to tree,

Nibbling in your canopy.

Wake up, *Leaping Legs*.

Clouds are drifting

Season's shifting

Croon a song of love and cuddles.

Splash about in rainy puddles.

Wake up, *Red Tails*.

No more dreaming
Sun is beaming
Nuzzle Mama in your den.
Frolic out in wooded glen.

Wake up, *Downy Feathers.*

No more lolling
Blue skies calling
Step into the morning light.
Spread your wings in fledgling flight.

Springtime, *Wee Boots!*

Perfect weather
Time together
Wonder's blooming all around.
Take in every sight and sound.

All the woodland's in full swing,

welcoming the joys of spring!